Mill City Santa's
Christmas Ride

Ronald DiBerto

Copyright ©2023 *Ronald DiBerto*

All Rights Reserved

Acknowledgments

I would like to acknowledge the City of Lowell, Massachusetts for helping me be the best Santa I can be.

As well as to all those within my Church for their support and involvement in helping me to be a Godly-focused Santa Claus.

Dedication:

This book is Dedicated to Rita MacDonald. She had a love of Christmas and for those around her.

1933 – 2022

" Go To Haverhill "

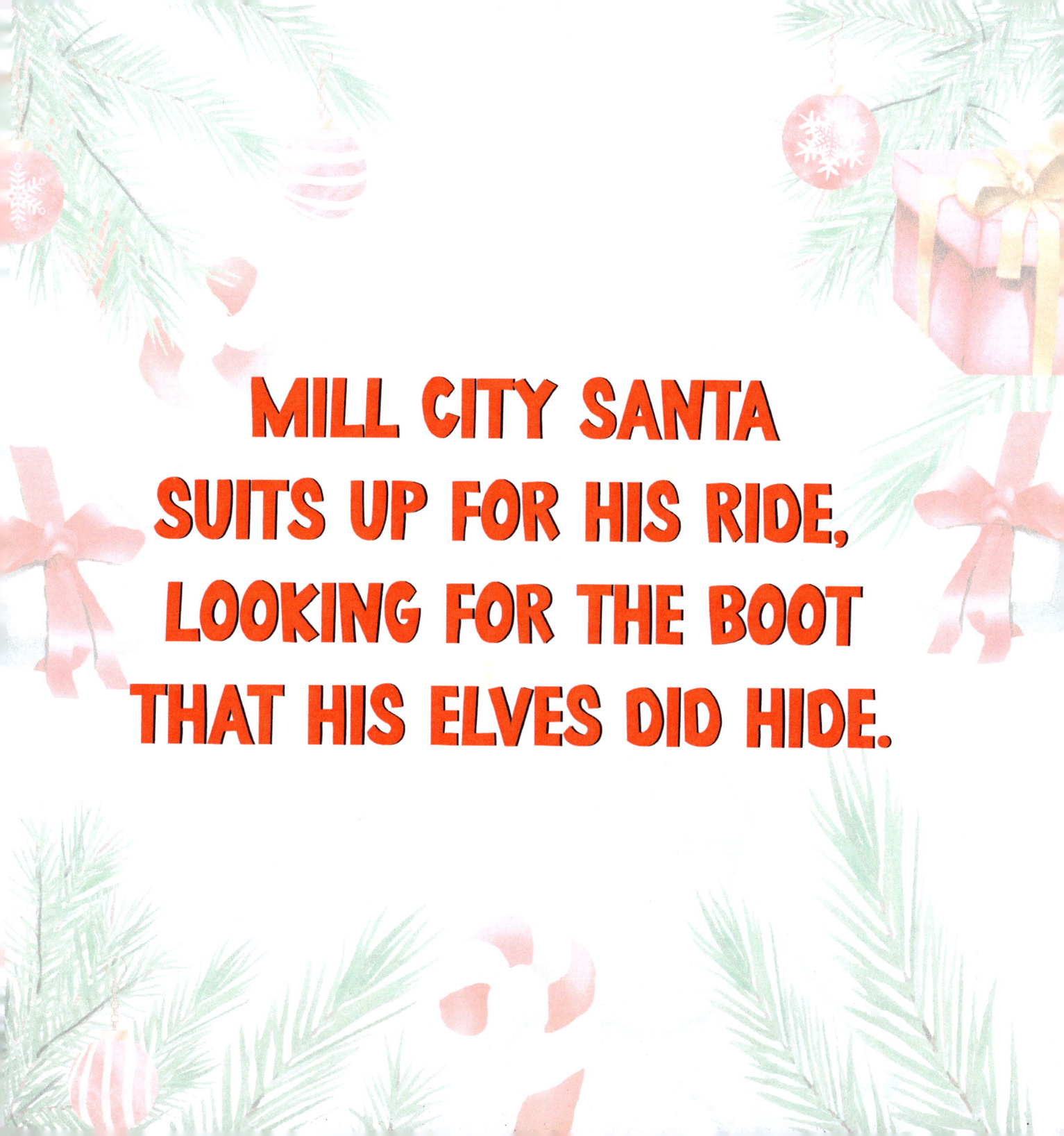

MILL CITY SANTA
SUITS UP FOR HIS RIDE,
LOOKING FOR THE BOOT
THAT HIS ELVES DID HIDE.

HE PUTS ON HIS COAT
AND A BIG RED HAT,
HE HUGS HIMSELF TIGHTLY
AND PURRS LIKE A CAT.

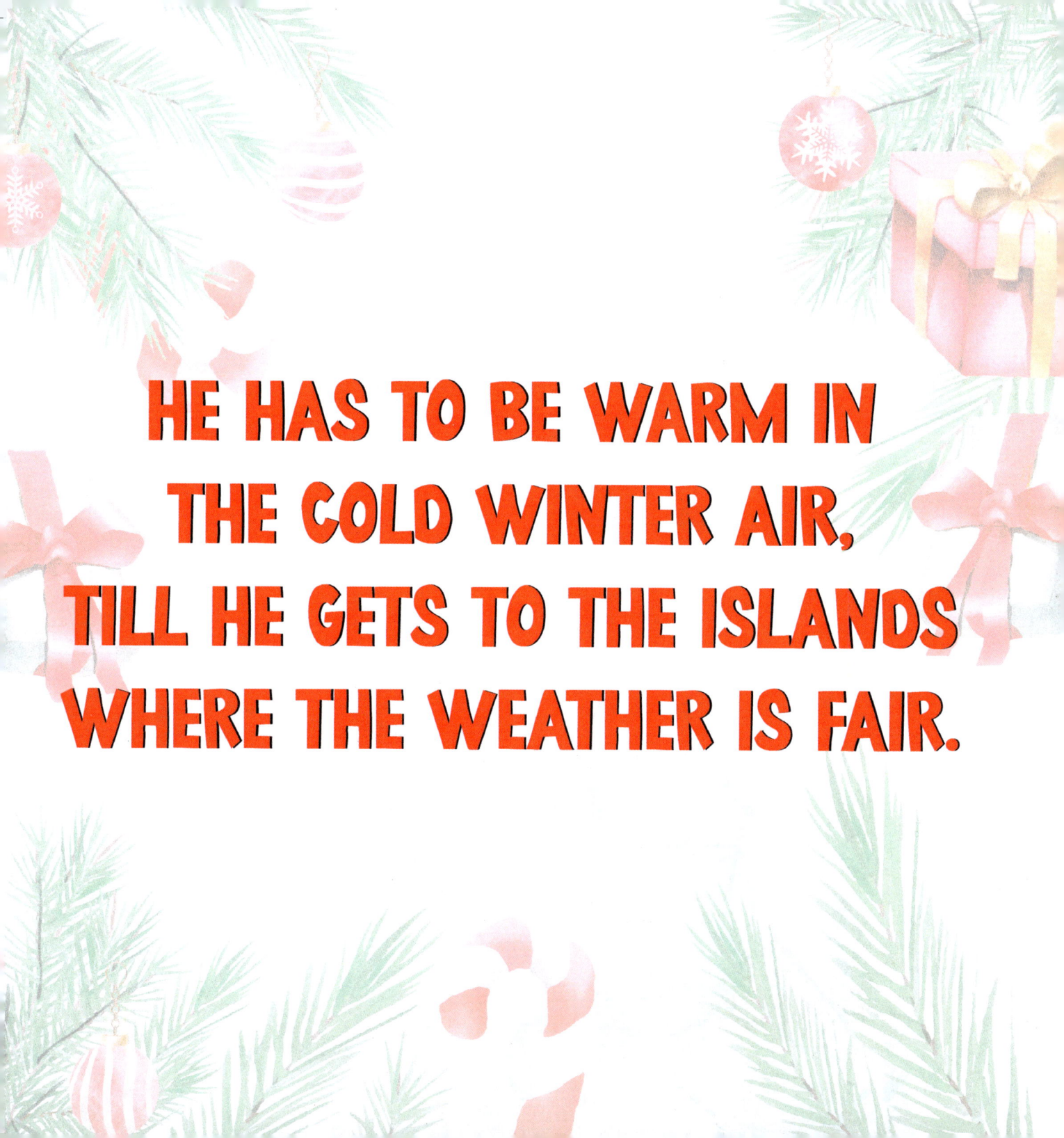

HE HAS TO BE WARM IN THE COLD WINTER AIR, TILL HE GETS TO THE ISLANDS WHERE THE WEATHER IS FAIR.

MRS. CLAUS BRINGS HIM
SOME SOUP AND HIS BOOK,
TO HAVE SOME LUNCH
AND A REALLY GOOD LOOK.

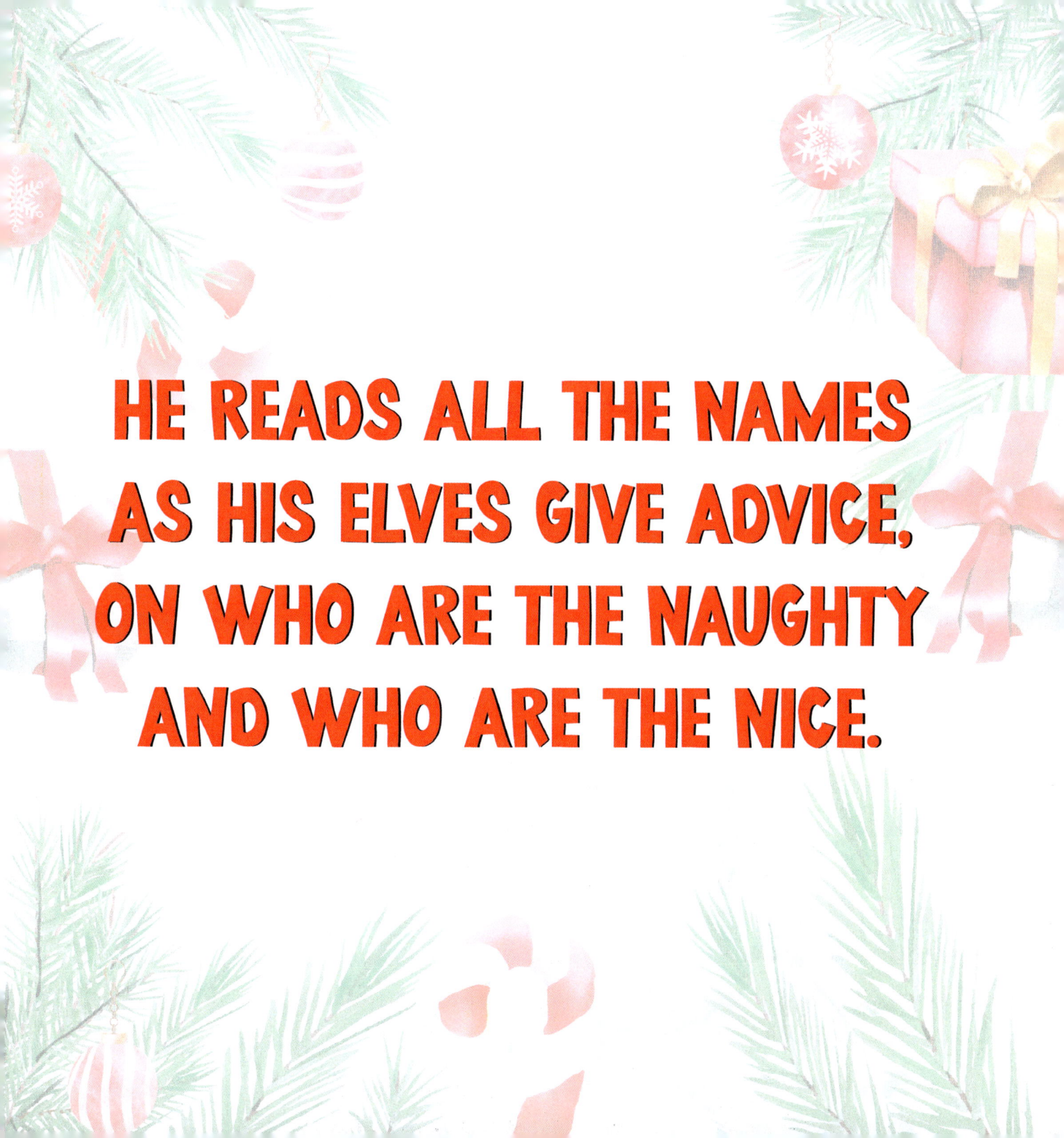

HE READS ALL THE NAMES
AS HIS ELVES GIVE ADVICE,
ON WHO ARE THE NAUGHTY
AND WHO ARE THE NICE.

HE CALLS HIS REINDEER BY ALL OF THEIR NAMES, TAKING THEM FROM THEIR REINDEER GAMES.

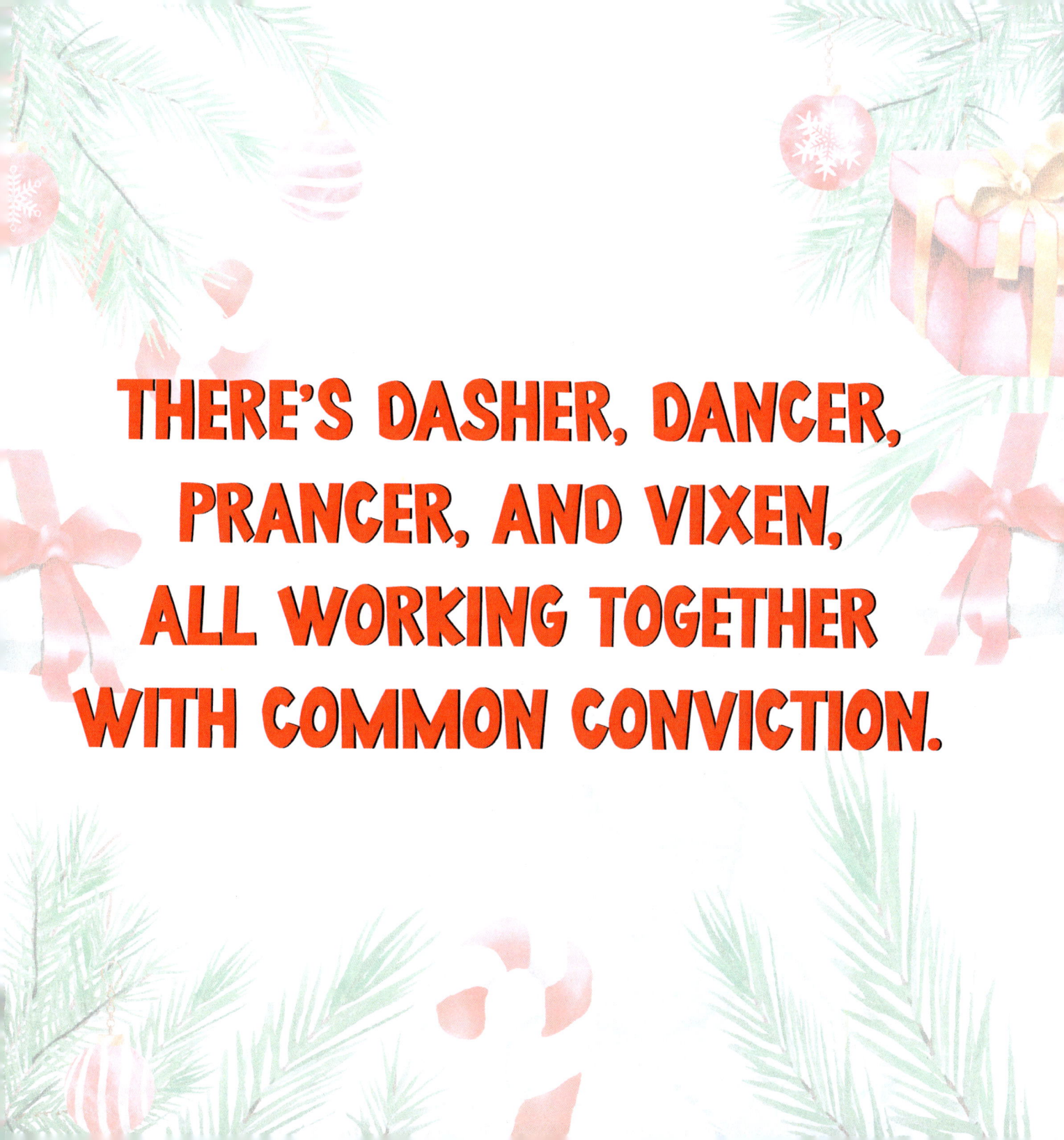

THERE'S BLITZEN,
COMET, CUPID, AND DONNER,
MAKING DREAMS COME
TRUE WITH LOVE AND HONOR.

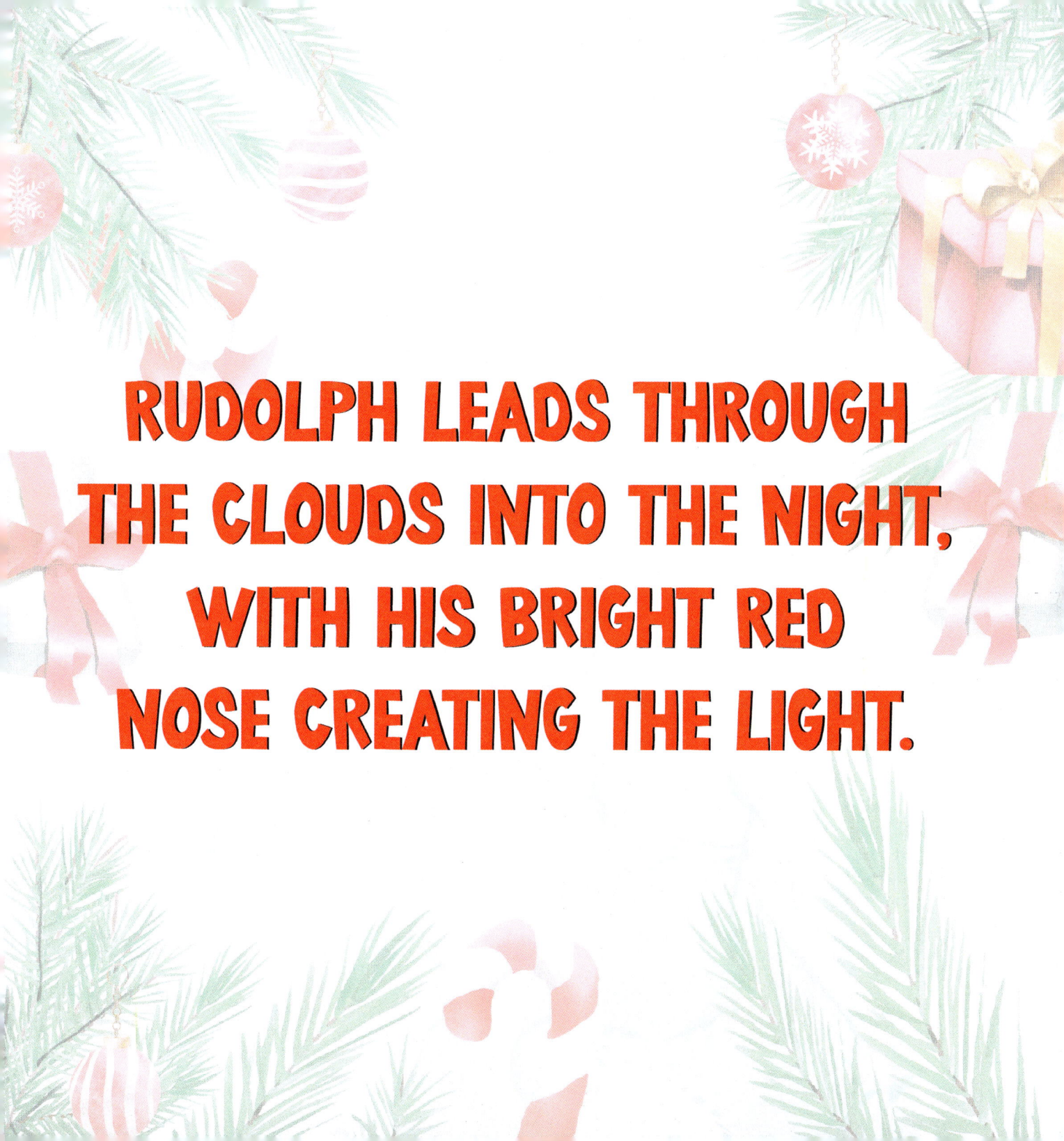

RUDOLPH LEADS THROUGH THE CLOUDS INTO THE NIGHT, WITH HIS BRIGHT RED NOSE CREATING THE LIGHT.

AS WE SAIL ACROSS THE BIG OPEN SKY, WITH A FLASH OF RED WE ALL FLY BY.

GOING OVER COUNTRIES, CITIES, AND STATES, DELIVERING TOYS, GAMES, AND SKATES.

SO IF YOU HEAR SOME BELLS AND MAYBE SOME CLATTER, AND YOU WANT TO GO SEE AS TO WHAT WAS THE MATTER,

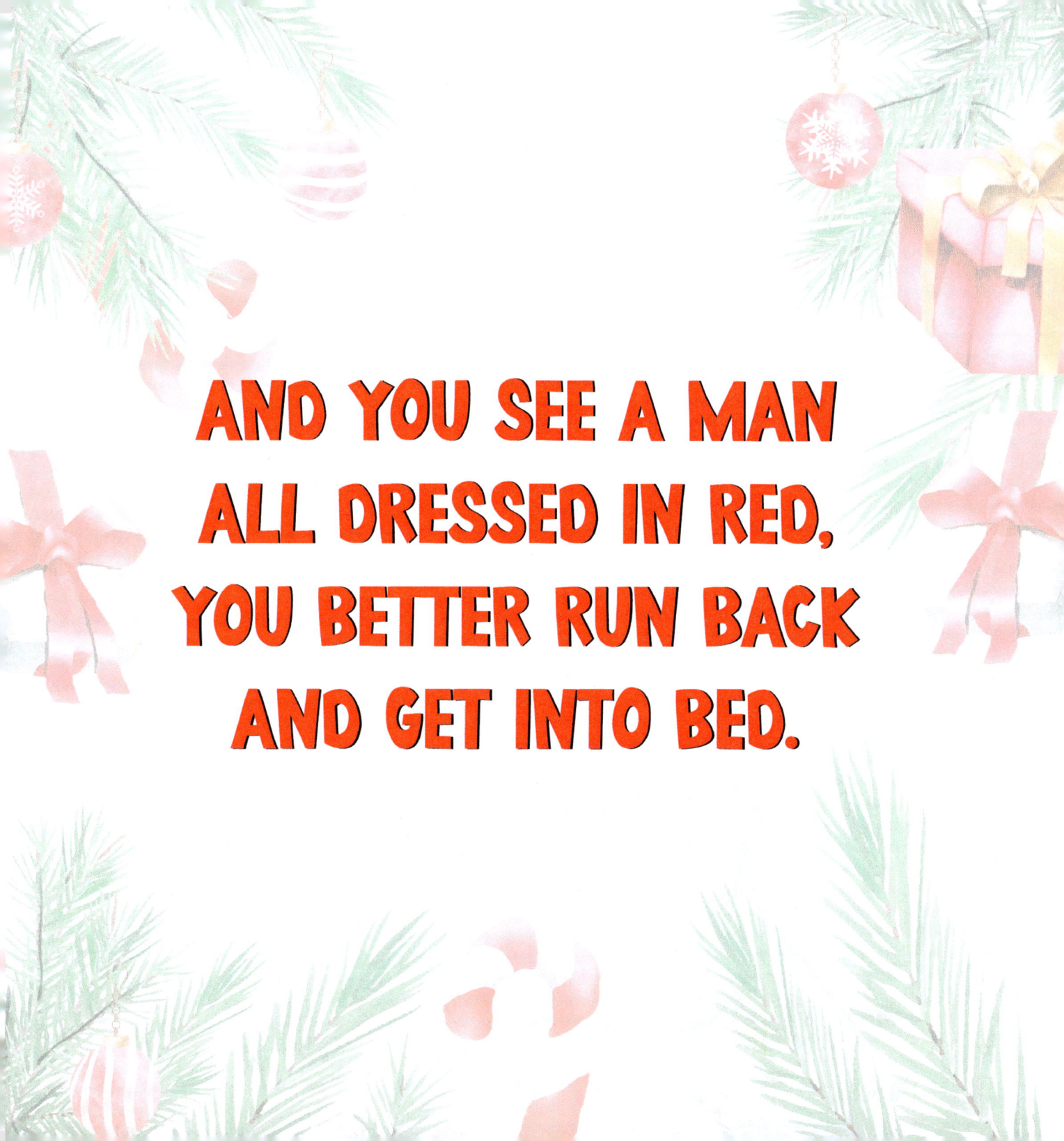

AND YOU SEE A MAN ALL DRESSED IN RED, YOU BETTER RUN BACK AND GET INTO BED.

BECAUSE HE KNOWS WHEN YOU'RE SLEEPING AND WHEN YOU'RE AWAKE, AND SEEING HIM TOO EARLY WOULD BE A MISTAKE.

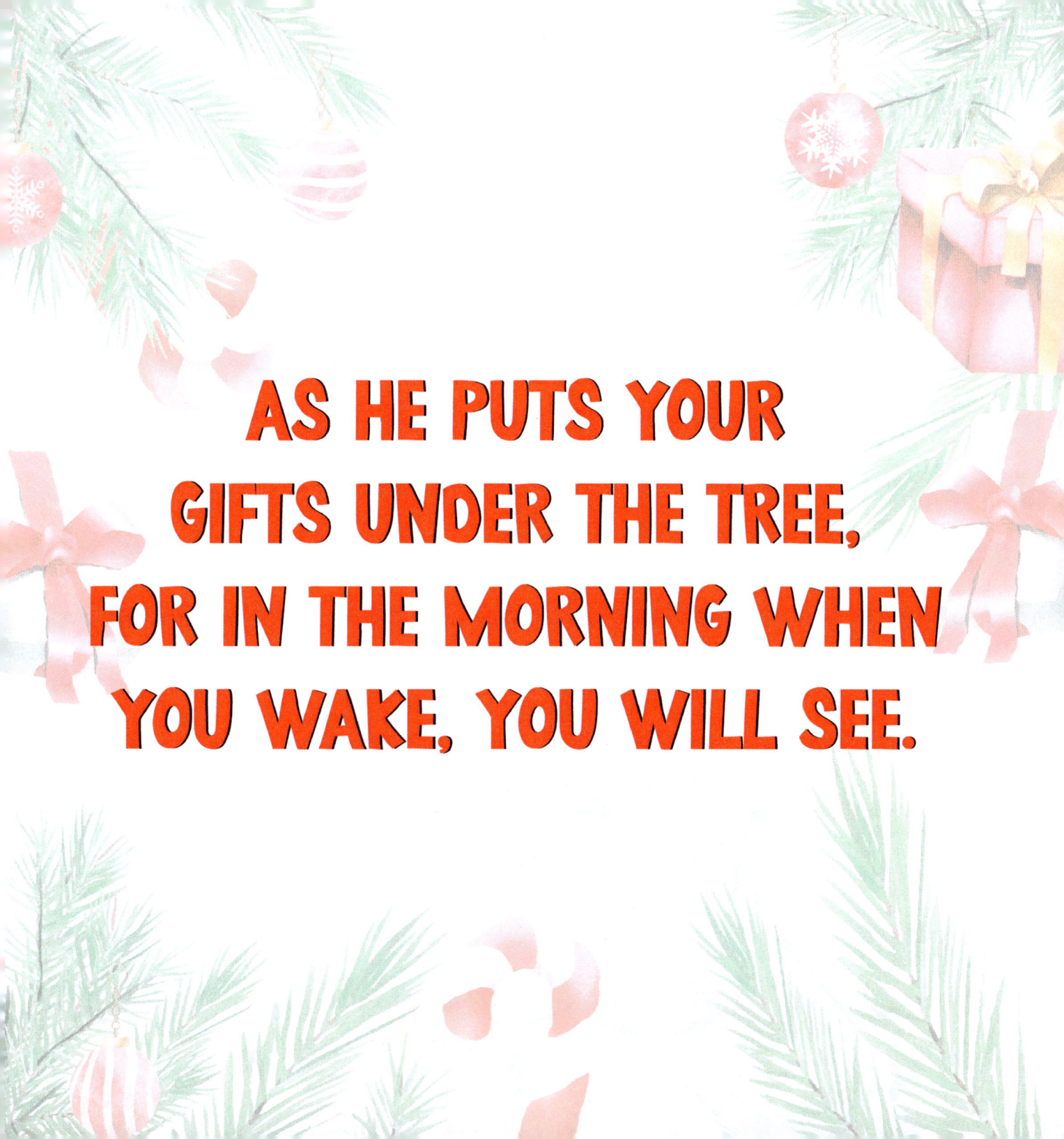

AS HE PUTS YOUR GIFTS UNDER THE TREE, FOR IN THE MORNING WHEN YOU WAKE, YOU WILL SEE.

**AS YOU RUN DOWNSTAIRS
AND LOOK WITH PRIDE,
THAT HE DELIVERED YOUR GIFTS
ON HIS CHRISTMAS RIDE!**

Made in the USA
Middletown, DE
06 December 2024